Published by Totally Unique Thoughts®
A division of TUT® Enterprises, Inc. Orlando, Florida
http://www.tut.com
Manufactured in China.
10 9 8 7 6 5 4 3 2 1
Collector's Edition First Printing
ISBN: 978-0-9814602-8-4

Your Magical Life

written by Mike Dooley

illustrated by Virginia Allyn

Long before there was even
sand in the hourglass, there
was a teeny tiny dot - so small
it was almost invisible - and it
was given to you as a gift.

At first puzzled and surprised,
you thought it was a joke, yet
trusting and curious, your
intuition led you to accept it,
and then to carefully examine it.

After becoming very teeny, tiny yourself, you were amazed to find an entrance to this little treasure! From which extended a long and winding checkerboard path.

Welcome to the
Jungles of Time and Space.
Where nothing is as it seems,
yet all things are possible.

Welcome to the
Jungles of Time and Space,
where nothing is as it seems,
yet all things are possible.

So inside you went,
finding yourself in an
ancient grove of bending
oak trees, under a bright
lemon sky, whereupon you
came across a sign ...
and then another ...
and another ...
and another ...

Love Always wins!

It doesn't matter where you've been... What matters is where you're going.

Miracles usually happen before you see them ... ...which means one may have just happened to you!

Never give up!

IT WON'T MATTER WHAT OTHERS THINK OR SAY...

YOUR THOUGHTS WILL BECOME THINGS...

AND YOUR WORDS WILL GIVE YOU WINGS.

Believe in
your dreams
so that they
can come true!

Goodbyes are never forever.

Ask a lot
of questions.
OK?

It doesn't matter if you get scared. There's still nothing you can't do.

Eventually you came to a large, round stone and on it was a big, shiny gold key, as if it was put there just for you.

You hesitated, but decided that since the dot was given to you, the key was probably yours, too. So... picking it up, you continued walking.

Rounding a corner, under a tree,
across a stream, and on a great hill,
you arrived at a big, locked gate...

Should you ever feel
lost or alone, forget not
from where you have come
and remember the signs.

Looking carefully between the
wrought iron bars, you could see
the entire Milky Way Galaxy and
one hundred billion galaxies beyond it.

Your heart raced, your imagination ran wild,
and you felt a little scared as you raised the
key to the steely lock, slowly slipped it in, and
gently turned it until you heard a very loud CLICK...
followed by a bright flash of light and a blast of trumpets!

Whereupon, seemingly light-years later, but, in fact, no longer than an instant... you found yourself living on the most beautiful little planet, having a wonderful life, a wrinkle of curiosity on your brow, reading these very words, in this very book, right here and now!

WOW!!!!! You did it! Great job!

IMAGINATION IS YOUR KEY!